DICK TURPIN

Legends and Lies

TERRY DEARY

With illustrations by
Stefano Tambellini

First published in 2007 in Great Britain by
Barrington Stoke Ltd
18 Walker Street, Edinburgh, EH3 7LP

www.barringtonstoke.co.uk

This edition first published in 2014
Reprinted 2017

A CIP catalogue record for this book is available
from the British Library upon request

Contents

Chapter 1
The Crowd

Saturday 7th April 1739, York

I remember the day Dick Turpin died.

Crowds filled the twisting streets of York City. They dressed in their best Sunday clothes and marched out of the city gates. They gathered in the fields outside the walls. They met at the scaffold where Dick Turpin would die.

I got there early so I was near the front of the crowds. The scaffold was built of rough wood and I was pushed into a corner right beside it.

A stout woman in a green satin dress shook my arm. "You're too young to be here," she panted. I could tell from her voice that she wasn't from round here. She came from the south.

"You're never too young to watch a hanging," a farmer said. His hands were stained with soil and his clothes smelled of cow muck and hay.

"My father said I had to come," I told the woman. "He said I had to watch Dick Turpin hang. Dad said I'll see what happens to villains. It will teach me a lesson I'll never forget!"

"Dick Turpin's not a villain!" an old man croaked. His voice was from the south as well.

People had come from all over England to watch this hanging.

A tall man, thin as a rope, gripped me by the ear. “Turpin was born a villain and he will die a villain,” he said. The tall man had glasses on the end of his nose and he wore an old black suit. “I taught him when he was a boy. I know.”

The farmer, the woman, the old man and the tall teacher crowded into my corner by the scaffold for an hour. The last hour of Dick Turpin’s life.

The spring day was cool and showery. “You should be wearing a hat,” the woman fussed. “It’ll get warm before the day is done. You need the shade.”

“I haven’t got a hat,” I said shyly. My family was too poor for things like that. In the crowd the woman couldn’t see my feet. I was too poor for shoes.

The woman shook her head. The farmer sneered. "I work all day in the sun. It does me no harm."

"It has fried your brain," she snapped at him. She turned back to me. "If it gets too sunny you can stand in my shadow," she said.

That was kind. No one was ever kind to a boy like me. The woman had a soft face and white hands. "Is Dick Turpin really wicked?" I asked her.

"Of course not!" the farmer cut in. "He's a gentleman of the road!"

"You mean a thief!" the woman cried.

"A gentleman thief," the farmer told her.

"The boy should not be here," the woman went on. "To see a man die is a cruel thing. To see an evil man choke and go to Hell is not for a child."

"I'm not a child," I said.

"How old are you?" she asked me. "Twelve?"

I shrugged. "I don't know," I replied.

The farmer spat. "You say the lad shouldn't be here. But you've come a long way to see Dick Turpin hang. *You're* here, lady. Why is that?"

"Revenge," she said softly. "Revenge."

Chapter 2
The Villain

The farmer leaned against the rail of the scaffold. He slid down so his face was level with mine. His teeth were yellow-green and his breath smelled of old onions. He wrapped a dirty hand around my shoulder.

"Here, son, let me tell you about the time Dick Turpin robbed a robber!" he said.

I nodded and said nothing.

"Dick Turpin was a poor lad, like you," the farmer said. "The rich folk don't care about us. They give us nothing. If we want money we have to work from dawn till dusk. We have to break our backs for pennies."

"Or steal it, like Turpin," I said.

The farmer nodded. "He was a poor butcher boy in London, you know?" he asked.

I had seen the butchers' shops in the Shambles – a narrow street in York. The butchers killed cattle at the back of the street and put the meat in the shops at the front. The smell of blood filled your head when you walked down there.

"A dirty job," I said.

"Dick decided to make a little extra money," the farmer said. "He stole some sheep and cattle. He cut them up and sold the meat. He was only trying to make some money to live."

The teacher tapped the farmer on the shoulder. “Excuse me, but you look like a farmer,” he said.

The farmer peered at him. “I am,” he said. “Twenty cows and fifty sheep.”

“You would not be happy if Turpin stole your animals,” the teacher sniffed.

“That’s different!” the farmer said. “Now take your sharp and pointy nose and stick it in someone else’s business! I was telling the lad about Turpin.”

The teacher gave the farmer a hard stare and began to read a book. Don’t ask me what it was. I never learned to read.

The farmer turned back to me. “Well, after that, Dick Turpin turned to highway robbery. He got himself a pistol and hid in the trees by the Radcliffe Highway. He didn’t have to wait long before a stranger rode along. Turpin jumped out in front of him and waved the pistol. 'Stand and deliver!' he cried."

"Deliver what?" I asked.

The farmer frowned. "I don't know. Deliver his money, I guess. It's what highwaymen always say. Now, do you want to hear this story or not?"

"Yes, sir."

"Then shut up," he said. "Where was I?"

"Stand and deliver," I said.

"Ah yes ... stand and deliver. The man on the horse handed over a purse, then Turpin said, 'Give me that gold ring!' The man on the horse said, 'It's my wedding ring. My wife will be upset if I lose it.'"

"Turpin wouldn't care," the lady in green satin muttered.

"But Turpin *did* care!" The farmer chuckled. "He asked what he could do and that's when his victim said, 'Fire your pistol at me!'"

"The man wanted Turpin to shoot him!" I gasped, and hopped from one cold foot to the other.

The farmer smiled. "He wanted Turpin to put a bullet through his cloak. He wanted it to look as if he'd been in a fight and hadn't just handed over his wedding ring without a struggle."

"And did Turpin do it?" I asked.

"He did!"

"What happened then?" I asked.

"The man said, 'Now put a shot through my *hat*, please!' And Turpin said, 'I don't have a shot left in my pistol. I just fired it.' That's when the man drew a gun and pointed it at

Turpin. 'Ah, but I have a shot in *my* pistol,' he said. 'I will shoot you if you don't hand me my purse and ring!'" the farmer said.

I laughed. "Turpin was tricked! Did the law get him?"

The farmer shook his head. "That's the best part of the story. It seems the man he'd stopped was Matthew King … the famous highwayman!"

"Turpin tried to rob another highwayman?" I asked.

"He did. Of course, after that, the two men became great friends and they were the terrors of Epping Forest."

"Robbing the rich," I said. "Just like Robin Hood. Turpin was a real hero, then."

The lady in the green satin dress grabbed my arm and shook me. "He was a villain," she said. “Don’t believe the fool’s tales. He was the most cruel man to ride the roads of Essex.”

“He was a hero!” the farmer shouted.

The woman leaned forward till her nose was close to his. “It is easy for you to say. You have just heard the stories. You don’t know his victims.”

The farmer spat. “Oh, and you do, eh?” he said with a sneer.

“I do,” the woman said.

“Who were they then?” I asked.

“Me,” she said. She spoke to me but kept her eyes on the farmer’s face. “Turpin and his gang robbed *me*.”

Chapter 3
The Victim

The farmer pulled a face as if his green teeth were hurting him. "Dick Turpin? Hurt a lady?" he asked.

The woman in green satin looked at him. Her look was as cold as the wind that blows in from the York moors. "Turpin is a bully. He was one of the Essex gang," she said.

"I've heard of them," I said. "They broke into houses and robbed the owners."

The woman nodded. “There were at least six of them,” she said. “They kicked down doors at lonely houses. They put pistols to the owners’ heads. They made the owners show them where their money was kept. They carried off everything they could and smashed the rest.”

“That’s spiteful,” the farmer admitted.

“What did they do to you?” I asked.

The woman closed her eyes for a moment. “It was over four years ago. 1734. They broke down my front door and marched into my room. They all wore masks. They said they knew I had money hidden in the house. They said they would shoot me if I didn’t tell.”

“If they shot you then you would *never* be able to tell,” the teacher said.

The woman gave a faint smile. “That’s what I told them. So the leader of the gang – I think

it was Turpin – went over to the kitchen fire and threw some logs on. He told his men to pick me up and carry me over to the fire."

"No!" I cried.

"They held me over the fire and the leader said he'd roast me alive if I didn't talk," the woman went on.

"So you talked," the teacher said with a nod.

"No! I did not!" the woman said. "I said the gang could roast me if they wanted. It would be good for them to see it, I said. Because one day they would all roast in Hell!"

"Brave lady," the farmer said.

"Did they burn you?" I gasped.

The woman gave a sigh. "My son came home and he saw what they were doing. He told them where the money was. He thought

he was saving his mother's life." She shook her head. "The men found £100. They stayed to drink all my wine and eat all my meat."

"But you lived?" the teacher said.

"I lived in fear. I'm too afraid to ever sleep again. The shock and the horror still haunt me."

"That's why you want revenge?" I asked. "That's why you want to see Turpin die?"

The woman nodded. "I want to sleep in peace. I saw the rest of the Essex gang hanged in London. Turpin is the last."

She turned to the farmer. "*That's* the sort of man you called a hero, farmer," she said.

The farmer shook his head. "Yes ... I mean, no. I was just telling you the stories that I had heard about Turpin. There were other stories."

The teacher wagged a finger. "The story of Turpin killing Matthew King is a lesson to us all," he said.

"Matthew King? Do you mean the highwayman he tried to rob? The man in the story you just told me? Did he become his enemy?" I asked.

The teacher pressed his thin lips into a hard smile. "Matthew King was his *friend*! Turpin shot his friend. What sort of a man does that?"

"It was an accident," the old man beside us muttered.

But the teacher wasn't listening. He was looking inside his coat pocket. He pulled out a piece of newspaper.

"The real hero isn't Turpin," the teacher said. "It was an inn-keeper, who risked his life to arrest the highwayman Matthew King. The inn-keeper was called Richard Bayes. He

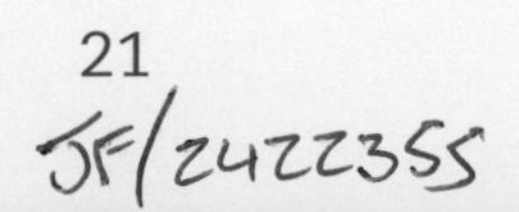

tracked Turpin to London and caught him in a stable." The teacher took off his glasses and cleaned them. Then he read the newspaper to us.

"Mr Bayes went to arrest King, but then King drew out a pistol," the teacher said. "He pressed it to Mr Bayes's chest and pulled the trigger. Luckily it didn't fire. King struggled to get out his other pistol, but it was tangled in his pocket. Turpin was near by, on horseback, waiting for King. King cried out, 'Shoot him, Dick, or we will be caught, by God!' Turpin fired his pistol and it missed Mr Bayes. He shot King in two places and King cried out, 'Dick, you have killed me!' When Turpin heard that, he left his friend and rode away as fast as he could. King died a week later from his wounds. But before he died he told everyone that Turpin was a coward."

The teacher folded the paper and put it back in his pocket.

The white-haired old man said, “Dick Turpin is no coward. Watch and see. He will die like a brave man.”

The teacher patted his pocket and smirked. “Turpin is a coward, sir. A coward,” he said.

Chapter 4
The Farmer

The farmer looked back up the road that came from York. “Not long now,” he said.

The crowd was bigger now. It pressed us forward onto the scaffold rails. I heard a soft rumble. It was like the distant roar of the River Ouse when it was flooding. It was the noise of the crowd cheering from a mile away down the road.

"It's Turpin," the teacher said, looking through his glasses and over the heads of the crowd. "Not long now."

The farmer looked at the woman. "You'll soon have your revenge then, lady."

"I wish I could push him off the ladder myself," she said.

The farmer rubbed a hand over his greasy hair and said, "In some ways I put Turpin there."

"Where?" I asked.

"I put him on the scaffold," he said. "He may be a great man, but Turpin's no match for John Robinson."

"John Robinson?" I asked. "Who's he?"

"Why, that's me, lad. I was the one that got Turpin arrested in York!"

"What did he do? Try to rob you?" I asked.

The farmer shook his head. "Have you not heard the story? I'm as famous as Turpin!"

"You?" I said and rubbed my eyes.

"Turpin shot Matthew King and ran off to Yorkshire where no one knew him," the farmer said. "And then he changed his name to John Palmer."

"We know that," the woman in the green dress said. "But I don't remember a story about John Robinson catching him."

"Then you should," the farmer said with a flash of anger. "Everybody in my village of Brough knows me."

"But we're not from your village," the teacher told him.

"I remember the day Dick Turpin rode past my farm," the farmer said. "He'd been drinking. I could tell. He was shouting and laughing with his friends."

"They'd been hunting," the old man with white hair said. "Harmless. A good day out. He was happy."

"His last happy day on earth," the teacher sneered.

"This is *my* story!" the farmer hissed. "Are you listening?"

"Yes, but be quick. I can see the cart with Turpin in it – he'll be here in a few minutes," the woman told him.

"Turpin rode through the village ... shouting and laughing ..." the farmer said.

"You've said that already," the teacher snapped.

"And that was when he saw a cockerel – it belonged to Francis Hall, the cow-man. The cockerel screeched at Turpin and he stopped laughing. He pulled out his pistol, walked over to the gate and shot it. I remember it well."

"So you said," the teacher said.

"Was that when you caught him?" I asked.

"No ... you don't go catching a man with a pistol, son. But I told him he'd have to pay for it. 'I saw you shoot that poor bird!' I told him. And you won't believe what he said to me ..." The farmer waited a moment.

"But you're going to tell us," the teacher said.

"'Wait until I load my pistol, then I'll shoot you too!' That's what Turpin said."

"So was *that* when you caught him?" I asked.

"Not exactly. I went to the law officer and reported what I'd seen. I told them John Palmer had killed Francis Hall's cockerel and *then* said he'd kill me!"

"So you didn't really catch Dick Turpin, did you?" I asked.

"I was the man that had Dick Turpin arrested. I should have the £200 reward."

The teacher shook his head slowly. "No, my friend," he said. "You did *not* have Dick Turpin arrested."

"I did – I tell you, I did!" the farmer yelled.

"No. You had *John Palmer* arrested," the teacher said, and he wagged his thin finger again.

"It's the same man. Dick Turpin *was* John Palmer," the farmer said.

"Ah, but nobody *knew* that," the teacher said. "Palmer was arrested. He would have paid a fine and then gone free. No, my farmer friend, the real hero in Turpin's tale is *me*!"

Chapter 5
The Traitor

The teacher took off his glasses and polished them on the sleeve of his old black coat.

"I should have the reward, you know," he told us. "Turpin had a price of £200 on his head. And they only caught Turpin because of me."

The old man looked at him, and his eyes were filled with hate. "Traitor," he muttered.

The teacher sniffed and turned his back on the old man. He looked at the lady in green satin and said, "Everyone in York thought Turpin was the horse thief, John Palmer. He was safe!"

"A horse thief could hang, of course," the lady said.

"Ah!" The teacher nodded and wagged his thin white finger. "But if they knew he was really Dick Turpin, then he would be hanged for sure. Oh, yes, I should have the reward."

"What did you do?" I asked. I shuffled my bare feet on the ground. They were freezing cold now.

The teacher sniffed at me as if I was a sour smell. His eyes were huge and round behind his glasses. "When he was in prison in York, Turpin wrote a letter to his sister. He sent the letter from York prison all the way home to Hempstead in Essex. He wanted his sister's husband to raise some money and set him free.

But her husband refused to pay the postage on the letter!"

I nodded. No one ever sent my family letters. We were happy about that. If someone sends you a letter you have to pay for it. We never had enough money. "So did *you* pay for Turpin's letter?" I asked.

"No. But I knew who'd sent it! I knew that writing. I taught Turpin how to write twenty years ago," he said.

There were pink spots in the teacher's winter-pale cheeks now. He turned back to the woman in the green dress. "I knew it was a letter from Turpin – the most wanted man in England. I took it straight to the law officer. Oh yes, upon my soul, I told him, 'That's the writing of Dick Turpin the highway robber.'"

The woman said, "And murderer, don't forget. He was wanted for murder too."

The teacher wasn't listening. His green eyes were glowing. "They sent me all the way up here to York," he said. "They showed me the prisoners in the jail and I knew him at once. I pointed him out." The teacher stretched out an arm – in his mind he was back in the prison. "'That's Turpin,' I said."

"And it was," the woman said with a sigh.

"Of course, at first Turpin tried to say I was a liar. He said he'd never seen me before. And so they found other people to say it was Turpin. But I was the first. Upon my soul, the very first," the teacher said.

"Traitor," the old man snarled again. "Giving away an old friend from school. What sort of gutter rat would do that?"

The woman in green frowned. "He was doing his duty," she said.

"My duty," the teacher agreed.

"You'll be happy to see him hang ... you gutter rat," the old man said.

"We *all* will," the woman said.

"*I* won't!" the old man told her angrily.

"So, why are you here?" she snapped back.

"To see a man die," he said. "A real man."

Chapter 6
The Old Man

The crowd roared and cheered as Turpin came into sight. Turpin nodded back bravely.

"He looks pale," the woman said. "That's fear."

The old man with white hair turned on her. "He has been locked in York Castle for months. He hasn't seen the sun in all that time," he said.

Today the pale sun was shining behind the thin April clouds. The teacher sniffed. "I hope

Turpin enjoys it," he said. "It's the last sun he'll ever see!"

Turpin's hands were tied. The guards helped him get down from the cart. They looked more afraid than Turpin. Five men in black suits watched silently. "They are the mourners," the farmer said.

"Are they Turpin's friends?" I asked.

The teacher sneered. "No. Turpin paid them to be here. They will guard his body."

"Guard it?" I asked.

"Oh, yes." The teacher nodded. "The doctors will want to claim the corpse once Turpin is dead. They will cut it up and show their students how the human body works."

"That would be a sin and a crime," the old man said. "The mourners will see the lad safe underground."

Turpin wore a rich new coat. "They say hundreds of people went to see him in prison," I said. "They gave him gifts, money and wine."

The farmer nodded. "He'll die a rich man!"

Turpin walked from the cart to the scaffold. He passed so close to us that we could touch him. The old man stretched out a hand and clutched the highwayman's sleeve. "Bless you, son!" he called.

The guards shoved the hand away and pushed Turpin towards the ladder. Turpin turned and called back to the old man, "It's a fine day to die, Father!"

The woman tried to move away from the old man, but the crowd was pressing too hard. "You are that villain's father?" she asked.

The old man nodded and raised his chin with pride. He looked down at me and rubbed my hair. "I remember Dick when he was a lad

like this. You see a thief and an outlaw. I just see my little boy."

"He was always a cruel bully in school," the teacher said.

The old man spat. "You taught him badly. And when he was caught it was *you* that betrayed him. I wish it was you up on the scaffold and not my son."

The teacher had no answer.

Turpin was shown the ladder and he placed a foot on the bottom rung. I could see that his leg was shaking. He stamped his foot on the platform to steady it and the crowd cheered.

"Say something!" a voice cried out.

Turpin turned and waited till a man in a black mask put a noose over his head. He climbed a few more steps. The crowd fell silent.

Turpin wasn't a handsome man. His face was marked by scars left by smallpox.

"I never meant to harm anyone," Turpin called out.

The woman in the green dress gave a snort of disgust.

"I only tried to make a living," Turpin shouted. "I wasn't born rich. I had to make my own way in life. I did the best I could. And now I go to a better place!"

"I hope you go to Hell," the woman in green muttered.

The crowd had just begun to cheer Turpin's bold words when he threw himself off the ladder.

I didn't see him die. I turned my head away.

The woman took my head and buried my face in the soft satin of her dress. I heard the voices muttering around me. The woman turned to the farmer. "You were wrong. You told the boy that you're never too young to watch a hanging," she said.

I looked up but kept my eyes turned away from the scaffold. The old man's face was as cold as iron. "They say revenge tastes sweet," he said softly. "Does it taste sweet to see my son die?"

The woman shook her head. "It tastes bitter. So bitter," she said.

The old man turned to the teacher. "And how does it feel to betray a man?" he asked.

"I was doing my duty," the teacher said.

"You taught my boy to read. He was the same age as this lad here," the old man said and touched my shoulder.

"Turpin gave me a lot of trouble in school," the teacher replied.

"Ah, so you betrayed him out of spite," the old man went on.

The farmer growled. "That's nasty, that is. A teacher should be kinder than that."

"And you?" the old man said. "You fool. You came to see a man die. You're no better." He turned and walked away from us.

Turpin's body was being loaded onto the cart and the crowd was drifting away. The old man waited for the cart to pass and began to walk behind it.

"Where are you going?" the woman asked all of a sudden.

"To the Blue Boar Inn," old Mr Turpin said. "My son will be laid out at the inn before his funeral tomorrow." He swayed a little as the cart with the body rolled past. I thought he was going to faint away.

"Take my arm, Mr Turpin," the woman said.

He nodded, silently. I watched as the two enemies walked off arm in arm.

The farmer rubbed his rough hands and gave the teacher a nudge. "That's not the end of Turpin. You'll see," he said. "That's not the end."

Chapter 7
The Body-snatcher

I didn't sleep. I lay shivering in the straw and listened to the rats in the darkness. Every time I closed my eyes I saw Turpin jumping off the ladder.

The stories of Turpin raced round York. My father came home that night, panting to tell the tale he'd heard.

"Do you know how Turpin escaped the law?" he asked me.

"He shot his friend Matthew King and then rode off to hide," I said.

"The story I heard was that Turpin did a robbery in London. He was spotted. So he jumped on his mighty mare – a horse they called Black Bess. He rode like the wind – and not even the wind could catch him. He was in York the next evening and he rode up to the Mayor of York! The Mayor! Imagine that!" my father said.

"But why would he do that?" I asked.

"When people said Turpin had robbed someone in London, the Mayor said it could not have been Turpin! How could Turpin be in London one day and York the next? The Mayor of York said no one could ride a horse as fast as that!"

"I've never heard of this Black Bess," I said.

"No, she dropped down dead at the end of the ride. But Turpin lived on. Oh, yes." Then my father said just what the farmer had said. "You haven't heard the last of Turpin."

But the next night, my father had another tale. As I lay in my straw I heard my father whisper to my mother, "They say the body-snatcher will have Turpin before the night is done!"

I didn't know what a body-snatcher was. But the word made me shiver too much for sleep. I got up from my bed and put a sack around my shoulders. I wandered into York to see the grave where Turpin lay.

It was in St George's churchyard. I had to see for myself. If Turpin was at rest, I thought, maybe *I* could get some rest too.

I peered over the churchyard wall and froze. There was a pale yellow light above one of the graves. At first I thought it was a spirit rising from the ground. Then I heard the soft scrape of wooden spades.

The yellow light was a lantern and the spades were the tools of the body-snatchers. I watched as they dragged the coffin out of the soil and quickly filled in the hole.

There were four men. They placed their spades on the coffin and raised it onto their shoulders. They walked to the gate and turned towards me. The man at the front held the lantern up to my face.

Suddenly he laughed. “I told you, boy. I told you it wasn’t the end of Turpin!”

In the pale glow, I saw the dirty face of the farmer who had stood at the scaffold. I smelled his farmyard smell.

“Where are you taking him?” I asked.

"To the surgeon. To Doctor Marmaduke Palms – he'll pay us well," the farmer said.

The men set off down the dark streets. I followed. I had the idea in my head that I would never sleep in peace again till Turpin's body was at peace too.

I saw the men take the coffin to a house on the edge of town. There they laid it in a shallow new grave in the garden. They went to the door of the house and vanished inside.

I turned and ran. Cobbles stung my bare feet and I slid over gutter mud and horse droppings. At last I reached the Blue Boar Inn and hammered on the door. A window opened. "Who's there?" someone shouted out.

"I want to see Mr Turpin!" I cried.

"He's not here any more. They hanged him yesterday and buried him this morning. Go away," the voice yelled.

"They hanged Dick Turpin's father?" I gasped.

"No. They hanged Dick Turpin. The body was brought here, but they took it and buried it again this morning," the person shouted back.

"I know ... but the body-snatchers just dug him up and took him to the doctor for cutting up," I yelled.

"They can't do that!"

"I know ... I want you to tell old Mr Turpin – to see if he can do something!" I cried.

"We'll do something, son. Wait there!" the voice told me.

The window closed. Lights flared in the inn and I could hear angry voices.

The rest of that night is as much of a nightmare as Turpin's leap from the scaffold ladder. A crowd of men and women carried flaming torches down the twisting streets. They followed me in a grim line as I led them to the doctor's gate.

The men at the front of the line pushed open the doctor's gate and began to scrape away the soil on the shallow grave.

The doctor poked his weasel head out of a window. "Who's there?" he asked.

"We've come for young Turpin, you foul monster. We're taking him back to his proper grave," a man roared.

"If you try to stop us you might end up in the same grave as my son!" old Mr Turpin added. The other men cheered him.

"Oh, no!" the doctor croaked. "I never wanted the body anyway! Take it and good luck to you. It's not my fault it's here. Let

Turpin rest in peace!" He slammed the window shutter and we heard bolts slide into place.

The line of people that went back to St George's churchyard was quieter now. Dick Turpin was laid to rest a third and final time.

I made my way slowly back to the Blue Boar Inn with old Mr Turpin leaning on my arm. He stopped at the door and turned. He wrapped his arms around me. "You did well, boy," he told me. "You did well. You have a good heart. My son would have done the same."

"Thank you, sir."

"Don't end up like him," he said, and his voice was breaking.

"No, sir."

"We can all rest now," he whispered.

I felt his warm tears falling on my head.

Legends, Lies ... and the Truth

The boy in this story is made up. But the people he meets in this book were real enough.

The stories of the body snatch and the rescue are true too. Doctor Palms was arrested.

Dick Turpin was held in York Castle and you can visit his cell in the Castle Museum.

Dick Turpin's grave can still be seen at Fishergate in York.

And Turpin really did shoot and kill his partner in crime, Matthew King. That's the truth.

He did escape the law in London. He did make a stupid mistake and get arrested for shooting a cockerel. That's the truth too.

He was betrayed by his old school teacher. Truth.

But people like stories of heroes. Over the years they began to add to Turpin's story. They invented a wonderful horse for him called Black Bess. Then they added a story that Turpin rode from London to York in a day to escape the law. Brave Bess dropped dead at the end. A lie ... or a legend?

Films and books have made Dick Turpin look like a gentleman. That's a lie. He was a cruel bully.

Dick Turpin died well ... but he lived badly. That's the truth.

Our books are tested
for children and young people by
children and young people.

Thanks to everyone who consulted on
a manuscript for their time and effort in
helping us to make our books better
for our readers.